S0-CWQ-506

"YOU KNEW TO DO the NEW shoe Bliee shoe

Will Bill

3 words -
BODS
MUSIC
AUTHORS
Think out the Box

IT DOESN'T MATTER WHERE YOU ~~POEM~~
AROUND the WORLD AND THEN BACK HOME
WE ALL HAVE SKIN, WE ALL HAVE GUTS

AND ALL OF WE ARE slighty NUTS

"YOU GOTTA LOOK AT THE BIG PICTURE."

A PAGE WITH NO POEM. "Sorry —
Now USE WORDS

1-15-00

IDEA — FROM MAKING Tuna SANDWICHES.

POEM

1st Half   2nd Half

POEM

12-27-99

PROBLEM: TOO MANY POSSIBILITIES —
to Stay FOCUSED ON
ONE thing & FOLLOW through

Metaone
Metatwo
Metathree
Metaphor

Anything AND ALL.

~~We Just can't Do IT ALL.~~

ANYTHING IS POSSIBLE,
Anything AT ALL,
Anything IS POSSIBLE,
Just can't do IT ALL.

there's something IN

Not the FROG
Not the ...
Not the Ifat
Not the Dog
either the Feline
Not the MOUSE
... who ...
Not the giraffe
Not the SNAKES!

11-2-07
Hi JEEM
HYGENE
(IT Card ...
on phone
at MFCA

Yeah!
one step at a tim

SPiNACH DiP PANCAKES

Kevin Kammeraad & FRIENDS

SPiNACH
DiP
PANCAKES

Kevin
KammeraaD
& FRiENDS

ISBN 978-0-9970476-0-8

Copyright © 2016 Kevin Kammeraad
Illustrations © 2016 Cooperfly, Inc.

All Rights Reserved.

Learn more about this book, the music,
and all the friends who contributed their creative talents at:
www.kevinkammeraad.com

Cooperfly Creative Arts, Inc.
3148 Plainfield Ave. NE, P.M.B. 248
Grand Rapids, MI 49525

Book production and design by Cooperfly, Inc.
Printed in Grand Rapids, Michigan at Color House Graphics
(HC) 10 9 8 7 6 5 4 3 2 1

Fristarts
Friends

Danny Adlerman
Kim Adlerman
Chris Fox
Alynn Guerra
Justin Haveman
Ryan Hipp
Stephanie Kammeraad
Carlos Kammeraad
Maria Kammeraad
Steve Kammeraad
Linda Kammeraad
Laurie Keller
Scott Mack
Ruth McNally Barshaw
Carolyn Stich
Joel Tanis
Corey Van Duinen
Aaron Zenz
Rachel Zylstra

IT DOESN'T MATTER WHERE YOU ROAM,
AROUND THE WORLD AND THEN BACK HOME.
WE ALL HAVE SKIN. WE ALL HAVE GUTS.
AND ALL OF US ARE SLIGHTLY NUTS.

A POEM
(AND TWO DRAWINGS)
FOR THE WOODWIND PLAYER

PICKLE HIGH.
PICKLE LOW.

SPINACH DIP PANCAKES

LAST NIGHT I MADE US DINNER.
WE'RE ALL A LITTLE THINNER.

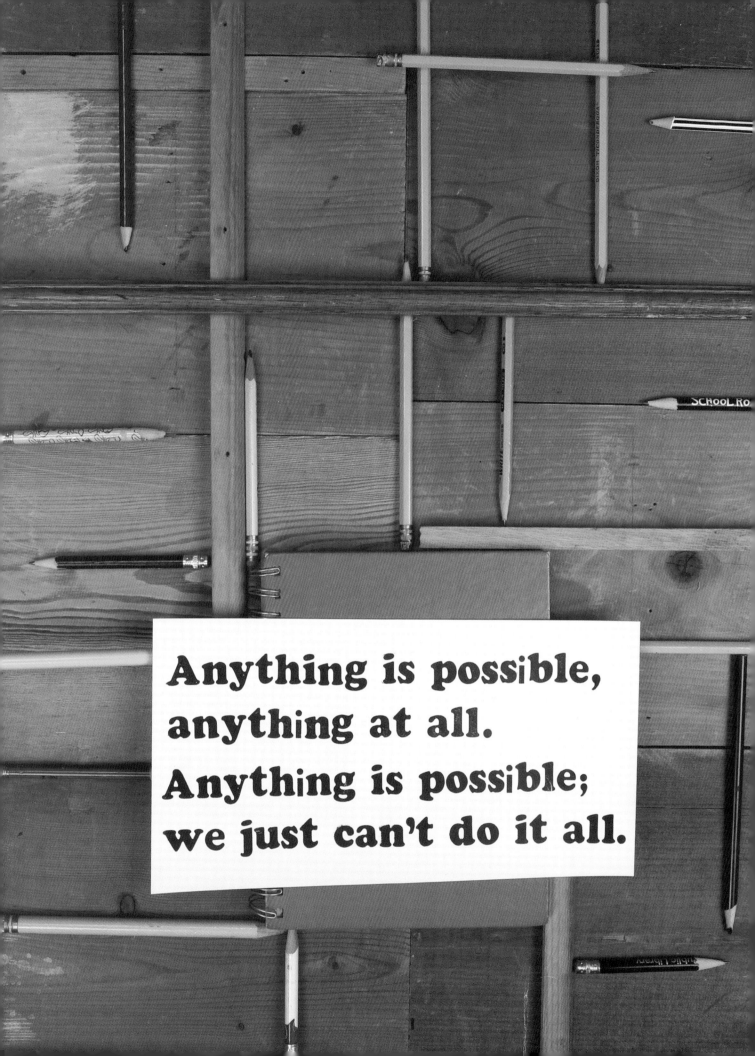

Anything is possible,
anything at all.
Anything is possible;
we just can't do it all.

I
HAVE A FEELING
IT WOULD BE QUITE
APPEALING
TO LIVE
ON
THE CEILING.

RUN-ON RHYMES

I DRY MY SLY TIE AND FLY BY BRUNEI.

BYE-BYE!

+ + + + + − + + +

+ +

$$10 - 1 = 9$$

YOU KNEW THE BLUE SHOE WHO FLEW TO THE ZOO, TOO?

+ + − + + + + + − + +

$$9 - 2 = 7$$

MOE, WILL JOE SEE YO' YO-YO SHOW?

YES!

+ + − + − + + + +

−

$$6 - 3 = 3$$

A Sea Cow?

A guinea pig is not a pig.
A hedgehog's not a hog.
A waterdog doesn't bark
Because it's not a dog.

A wombat is not a bat;
A numbat isn't either.
A jellyfish is not a fish,
Nor made of jelly neither.

A koala bear is not a bear.
A sea cow's not a cow.
Who chose these names anyway?
I'm so confused right now!

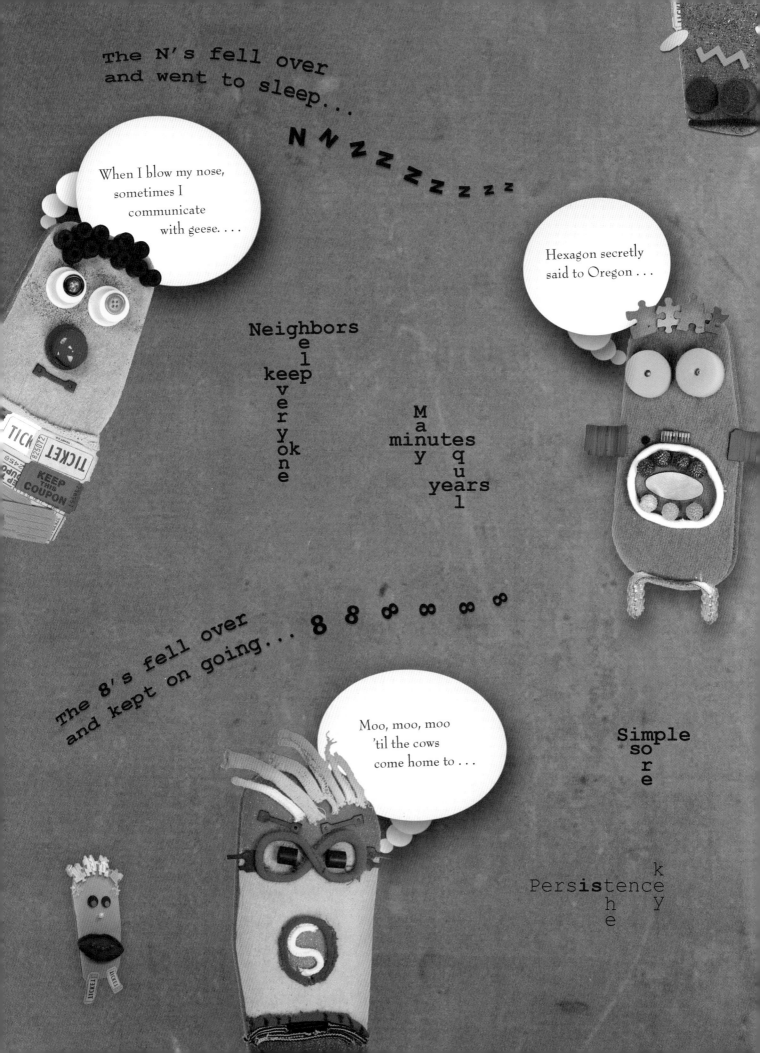

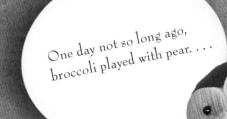

One day not so long ago,
broccoli played with pear. . . .

b   c
r   h
i   a
n   n
g   g
Complaining   e
n
g
s

D
i   y
v
different   r
t
always   equal

Each
o
u
offers
s
o
m
e
t
h
i
new   n
g

The O's fell over
and no one noticed...

O O O O O O O

"Please don't pet the peas,"
said Mom. . . .

Mother
h
a
n
k   for
you
l

Aardvark

Mississippi

Hat

I WAS STROLLING DOWN THE STREET
WITH MY FRIEND AARDVARK. SUDDENLY,
MY HAT FLEW OFF AND IT FLOATED FAR AWAY.
WE JUST KEPT ON WALKING
AND FOUND IT IN MISSISSIPPI.

A STORY
INSPIRED BY
THREE WORDS,
TOLD IN
THREE SENTENCES

INQUIRING MINDS

I WAS WONDERING,
IF A TREE FALLS IN THE WOODS,
DOES IT MAKE PAPER?

I'M CURIOUS TO KNOW,
DO NUMBERS KNOW THEIR NEIGHBORS?

HAVE YOU EVER WONDERED,
IS THERE ANOTHER WORD FOR THESAURUS?

DOES INK CAPTURE INKLINGS?

CAN WE FIND ART IN THE EARTH?

ARE WE CONSCIOUS OF OUR CONSCIOUSNESS?

SHOULD I CHANGE MY HAT?

DO WALLS KEEP US IN OR OTHERS OUT?

IS HERE BETTER THAN THERE?

IF A COW PATTY IS "POO," WHAT'S A CHICKEN PATTY?

WHY DO WE TALK SO MUCH, BUT SAY SO LITTLE?

WHAT'S FOR BREAKFAST TODAY?
YES, LET'S START THERE.

Public Library
GRAND RAPIDS, MICH.

760.27

This book may be kept FOUR weeks (unless it is designated a Seven Day Book); the fine if it is kept longer is two cents a day.

No book loaned to anyone having fines or penalties unsettled.

Borrowers will be held responsible for imperfections of book, unless the same are reported when the book is taken.

Extract from the State Library Law.

Sec. 1.--Any person who shall tear, deface or mutilate, or write upon, or by any other means injure any book, pamphlet, map, or other printed matter, or picture, belonging to, or loaned to, any public library, shall be deemed guilty of a misdemeanor, and punished by a fine of not less than two dollars or more than one hundred dollars, or by imprisonment not more than sixty days.

KEEP YOUR CARD IN THIS POCKET

F28-50M-10-30

GRAND RAPIDS PUBLIC LIBRARY

3 1906 8381 3076

Ja 13 '33 F M

Pg 11. Mr. Tolsh contemplates jellyfish.

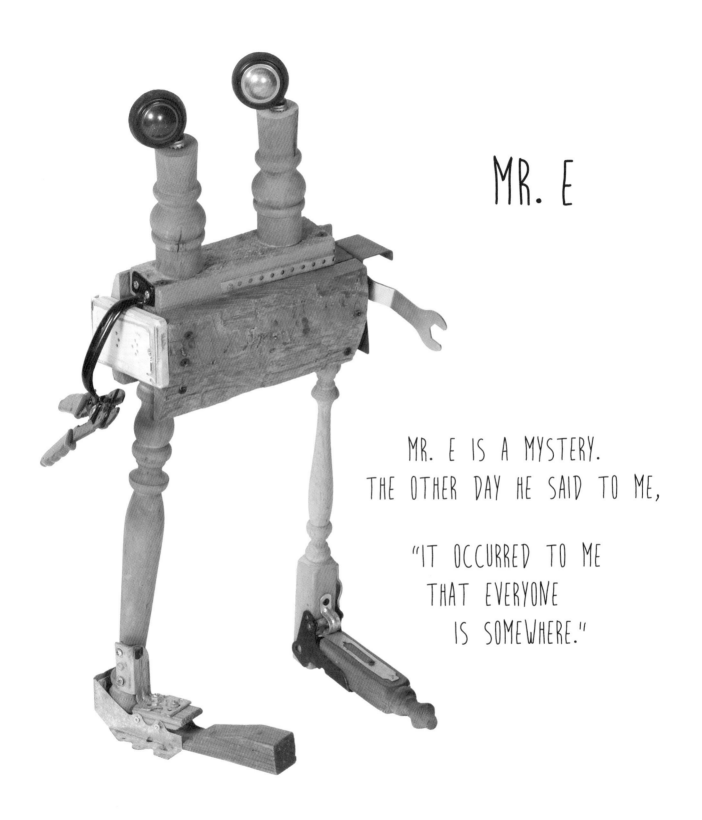

MR. E

MR. E IS A MYSTERY.
THE OTHER DAY HE SAID TO ME,

"IT OCCURRED TO ME
THAT EVERYONE
IS SOMEWHERE."

"Weitherd Words"

HIGHWAY

WASLAND ISLAND

ENO

CRAYOFF

SIDERUN

SIDEWALK

CRAYON

SODOWN

LOWAY INJURY OUTJURY

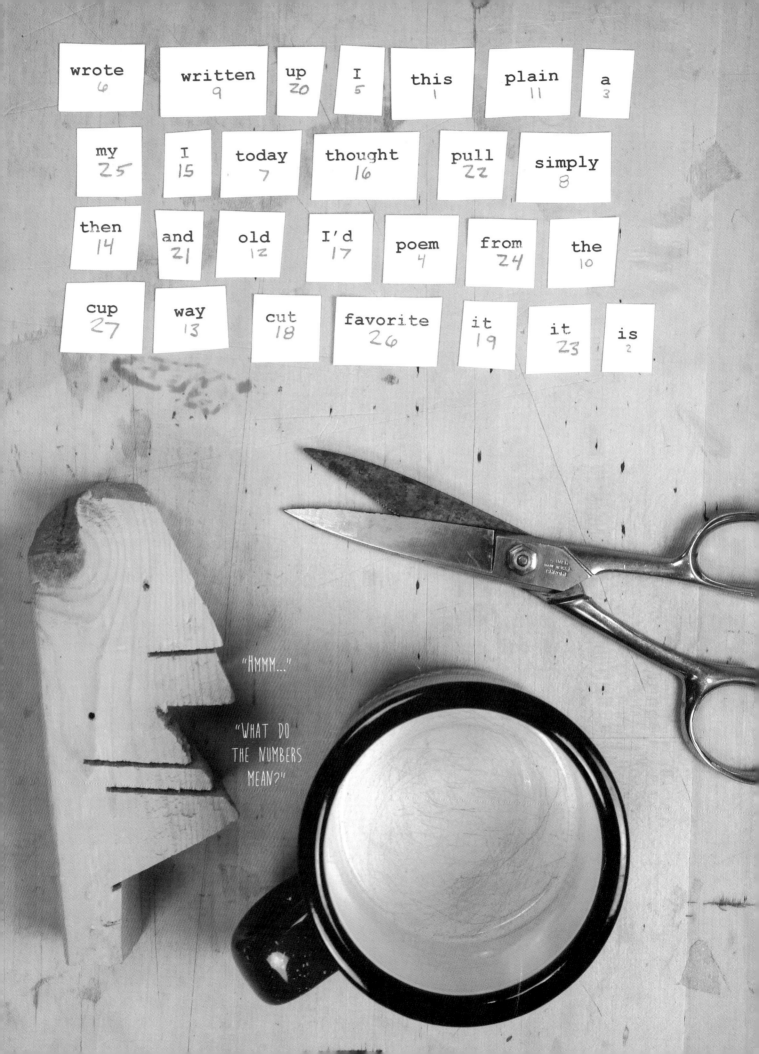

YOU'RE GREAT, YOU'RE SWELL

(SONG FOR SOMEONE YOU LOVE)

I LOVE YOU IN THE MORNING

I LOVE YOU IN THE NIGHT

I LOVE YOU ALL THE TIME

'CAUSE YOU'RE ALRIGHT.

YOU'RE ALWAYS ON MY MIND

EVERYWHERE I GO

'CAUSE I LOVE YOU...

YO, YO, YO.

YOU'RE GREAT.

YOU'RE SWELL.

YOU DON'T EVEN SMELL.

you can call me BOO LOU

You can call me BOO LOU TOO

WHO FOUND IT?

IT WAS NOT THE FROG
WHO FOUND THE HAT.
IT WASN'T THE BIRD
AND NOT THE... FELINE.

IT WAS NOT THE MOUSE
AND NOT THE ANTS.
IT WASN'T THE GUY
IN FANCY... TROUSERS.

IT WAS NOT THE LOBSTER
AND NOT THE GOAT.
IT WASN'T THE KID
IN THE COLORFUL... JACKET.

IT WAS NOT THE DOG
NOR WAS IT MORRIS.
IT WASN'T THE PIG.
IT WAS THE SAURUS!

Anything is possible, anything at all. Anything is possible;

don't have to do it all.

Wonder Canoe

(a found poem)

the

stories

are found

at the edge of

the

wonder

canoe.

But slow down,

hear,

the song of the

sparrow.

I'm bored.

Anything is possible, anything at all. Anything is possible; just listen for your call.

TOP NOTCH
SPINACH DIP PANCAKES*

TONIGHT I MADE US DINNER.
THIS ONE IS A WINNER!

* With peanut butter, kale, artichoke, almond, red raisin, garlic, apple, cinnamon, raw honey, cashew, avocado, red pepper, maple syrup, cheddar cheese (would you please), and a banana on the side.

THE POSSIBILITY OF ANYTHING

THE IDEA
IN MY MIND,
FOR THE ILLUSTRATION
OF THIS PAGE,
IS
SIMPLY
STUNNING.

IDE
A
EVERY

AS

RE:

WHERE